Book Club Edition

WALT DISNEY PRODUCTIONS
presents

Country Mouse, City Mouse

Random House   New York

Abner was a little brown mouse.
He lived on a small farm in the country.
He did not have much money.
But he loved his happy country life.

Each morning he watered his garden.

Then he clipped
his hedge . . .

hoed his corn . . .

and tied up
his tomato plants.

After the work was done, Abner walked down to the stream, carrying his fishing pole and a can of worms.

While he waited for a fish to nibble, he often fell fast asleep.

But if a fish suddenly tugged at his line,
Abner woke up fast!

And he carried
the fish home for dinner.

On his way home
Abner always looked in his mailbox.
One day he found a letter inside.
Abner tore open the envelope and read
the letter.

"FRIDAY!" cried Abner.
"That is today! Monty
will be here any minute!"

Abner raced into the house.
There was no time to lose.
He wanted everything to be ready
when his city cousin arrived.

First, Abner dusted the furniture.

Next, he swept the floors.

After that he beat all the dirt out of the rugs.

Then Abner gathered
all the dirty dishes
on a tray.

He dumped them into a sink filled
with soapy water and scrubbed them clean.

Abner picked fresh vegetables from his garden and made a delicious summer salad.

He cleaned the fish he had caught, and put it into the oven to bake.

Then Abner made some of his special pie dough.
Soon the spicy smell of hot apple pie filled
the kitchen.

Just as Abner
was taking the last pie
out of the oven, he heard
a loud honking outside.

Monty had arrived in a bright-red sports car.
He was wearing his fancy city suit.
Abner ran out onto the porch to meet his cousin.

"Come into the house," said Abner.
"You are just in time for dinner."

Abner was very proud of his dinner.
He told his cousin how he had grown
all the vegetables and caught the fish.

Monty ate every bit of food on his plate
and then asked for more.

During dinner Monty talked about his exciting
life in the city.

"Country food is fine," he said. "But you have
to work too hard to get it. In the city I eat all
the best food and I don't even have to work for it."

After dinner,
the two cousins
went upstairs.

When they were tucked in bed, Abner said,
"I do like my country life. But city life
certainly sounds exciting."

"Why don't you go back to the city with me?"
Monty asked.

"Maybe I will," said Abner.

Home
Sweet
Home

Early the next morning, the two cousins
packed their bags.

Monty loaded the bags into the car.

Abner left extra food for the chickens
and the ducks and the geese.

Then he climbed into Monty's bright-red sports car,
and away they went.

Poor Abner!
He had never gone
so fast before!
He had to hold on to
his hat to keep it
from blowing away.

"Isn't this the life!" said Monty.
"We will reach the city in no time.
You will love it, I know."

The closer they got to the city,
the more cars they met.

But Monty did not seem to mind.

He zigged and he zagged, steering
around the giant cars and trucks.

Abner coughed and choked.
He had never seen so much smoke
or heard such a lot of tooting.

At last Monty
parked his car.
"Here we are!"
he shouted.

Slowly they climbed the steps
to the door of a huge
town house.

Then they slipped through the mail slot
into the front hall.

The floor was so shiny that Abner could see
himself in it.

Suddenly a terrible, roaring machine came
sweeping straight toward them.

It was eating up everything in its path.

"HELP!" shouted Abner.

Monty grabbed
his cousin and
pulled him into
another, bigger room.

"That was just a vacuum cleaner," said Monty. "Don't be afraid of it. Come on. . . . Let's eat!"

Monty led Abner up to the top of a long table. There the little country mouse saw the most wonderful feast he had ever laid eyes on.

"My goodness!" he said. "Just look at that!"
"I told you city life was great," said Monty.
"Eat as much as you like. It's all for us."

Abner did not know what to eat first.
He tried the olives and the cheese.
Then he had a shrimp on a toothpick.

After that the two cousins ate liverwurst
and noodles.

"Don't forget to save some room for dessert,"
said Monty.

Just as Abner was about to bite into a piece
of delicious-looking chocolate cake—
         E-E-E-O-W-R-R!
A ferocious monster of a cat appeared.

Up onto the table leaped the cat.
Down onto the floor jumped Monty and Abner.

"Follow me!" said Monty.

Together, they raced to the door of his mousehole.

Abner was so frightened he had to sit down.

"That was close," he said.

"Oh, that was nothing," Monty answered. "I'm used to cats."

When the cousins were quite sure the cat was gone, Abner said he must go home right away.

"But you just got here," said Monty. "We haven't even finished eating."

"I have had more than enough," said Abner.

He gave
his city cousin
a big hug.

Then Abner ran out of the house,
down the street, and into the road.

He raced straight home
as fast as he could go.

NEW
CITY

Abner's own snug bed in his own little house had never felt so good.

The next morning he woke up early and pushed open the windows.

Then he put on his clothes and went out with his old farm friends to watch the sun rise.

"I would much rather be a poor country mouse than live in fear in a rich city house," he said.